MW00748831

DreamWorks
BEE
MOVIE
™

HarperCollins®, ®, and HarperEntertainment™
are trademarks of HarperCollins Publishers.

Bee Movie: The Movie Storybook

For information address HarperCollins Children's Books,
a division of HarperCollins Publishers,
1350 Avenue of the Americas, New York, NY 10019.
www.harpercollinschildrens.com

Library of Congress catalog card number: 2007932786
ISBN 978-0-06-125179-5

Book design by Rick Farley and John Sazaklis
❖
First Edition

The Movie Storybook

Adapted by
Susan Korman

Pencils by
Artful Doodlers and Marcelo Matere

Digital Paints by
Dave McCaig

HarperEntertainment
An Imprint of HarperCollins*Publishers*

Barry B. Benson raced through New Hive City toward the outdoor ceremony. He buzzed into line.

"It's Barry Benson, college graduate!" greeted his best friend, Adam Flayman.

"We're not graduates yet . . ." Barry replied. "But after today, we're going to be the ones making honey in this hive!"

When the ceremony ended, Barry cheered. He was now officially a worker bee.

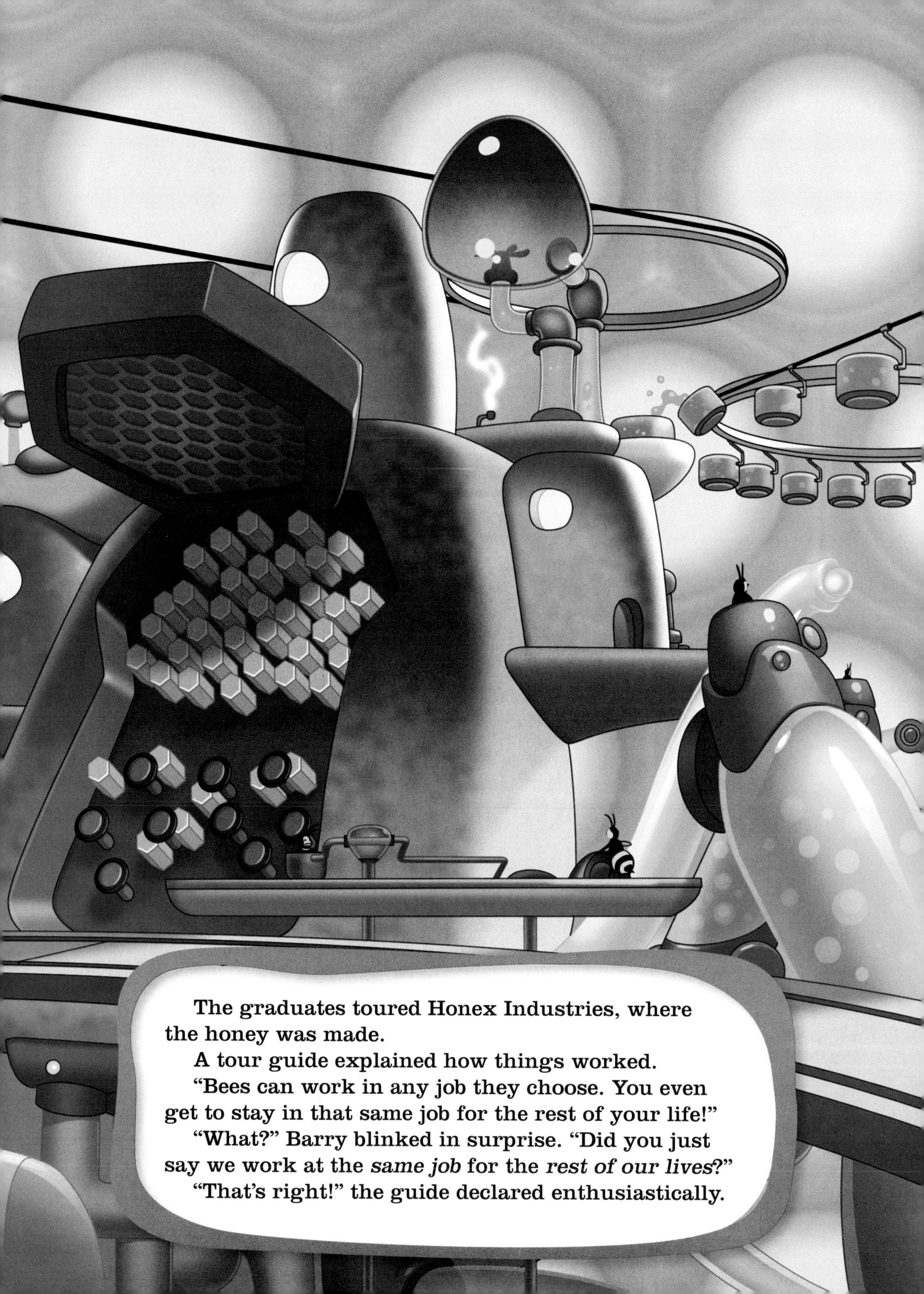

The graduates toured Honex Industries, where the honey was made.

A tour guide explained how things worked.

"Bees can work in any job they choose. You even get to stay in that same job for the rest of your life!"

"What?" Barry blinked in surprise. "Did you just say we work at the *same job* for the *rest of our lives*?"

"That's right!" the guide declared enthusiastically.

As Barry and Adam walked home, huge bees flew in. Pollen jocks! Their job was pollinating flowers.

"They get to travel *outside* the hive," Barry exclaimed.

The jocks knew a fan when they saw one and decided to have some fun. "We're collecting pollen tomorrow," one said. "It's a puddle jump for us, but maybe you aren't up for it."

Barry was! The next day he met the pollen jocks and was soon flying over the exciting Technicolor world of Central Park. He just had to remember one thing: Absolutely *no* talking to humans!

Barry and the pollen jocks landed on some bright yellow flowers that were actually . . . tennis balls!

"Help!" Barry called. "My feet are stuck!" Suddenly, a human picked up the ball and slammed it, bouncing Barry into a busy city street.

Then it started to rain—and bees cannot fly in the rain. He zipped into a nearby apartment window.

"A bee!" the humans inside screamed in terror, as one tried to smash Barry.

"Don't hurt him!" a kind woman yelled.

Gently, Vanessa carried Barry to the window. "There you go, little guy," she said, and set him free.

Barry knew he wasn't supposed to talk to humans, but he *had* to thank Vanessa for saving his life. Just the one time would be OK—right?
"Umm . . . hi!" he said. "I wanted to say thank you."
Vanessa was shocked. She dropped a stack of dishes. "You're a bee—and you're talking!"
Barry eventually convinced Vanessa she wasn't dreaming. They went up to her beautiful rooftop garden.
Vanessa told Barry she was a florist, and he told her about having to work at Honex for the rest of his life. They talked for hours.

Honey
Honey
Honey
Honey
Honey
Honey
Honey
Honey
Honey

Barry and Vanessa became fast friends.
One day they were at a supermarket when Barry spotted a whole aisle filled with honey.
"What in the world is *that*?" he demanded.
"People eat honey," Vanessa explained.
"What?" Barry was shocked. "That's stealing!"
He vowed to find out exactly how humans were doing it.
Honey
Honey
Honey

Barry discovered that beekeepers had trapped bees in fake hives and used a nasty device called a smoker to force them to keep making honey.

Back in New Hive City Barry told his family about the horrible things he'd seen.

"I, Barry B. Benson, intend to bring justice to the bees. I'm going to sue the human race!"

With help from his friends, Barry worked hard preparing his case.

One night Barry and Vanessa stayed up late studying law books while Adam slept.

Vanessa was worried. “Do you realize how big this is, Barry?” she asked. “Are you sure you want to go through with it?”

“Oh, I’m sure all right,” Barry answered. “When I’m finished, humans won’t be able to say, ‘Honey, I’m home,’ without paying us bees for it!”

VANESSA'S
FLOWERS
BUN
THE LAW OF
CIVIL PROCEDURE

On the day of the trial, Barry felt a chill as the defense lawyer, Layton T. Montgomery, strode past his table.

At first things went well. Then Montgomery laid a sneaky trap. He insulted and taunted the bees again and again.

Finally, Adam couldn't take it anymore. Just as Montgomery had planned, Adam flew out of his seat—and stung Montgomery.

"Help!" the lawyer cried, hamming it up for the jury. "I've been hit!"

Montgomery demanded that the case be dropped. “There’s no evidence of wrongdoing,” he told the judge.
“*Here’s* your smoking gun!” Barry declared. “Beekeepers use this thing to keep bees prisoners.”
“*That* harmless contraption?” Montgomery scoffed. He grabbed the smoker, accidentally pointing it toward the courtroom’s bee section, instantly knocking them out.
“Free the bees! Free the bees!” the jury chanted.
Barry and Vanessa slapped high fives. They had won their case!

ATFH

Immediately, all honey farms were shut down. Government agents destroyed the smokers and seized honey from restaurants, supermarkets—even bears.
Once people stopped eating honey, Honex had too much of it.
“Stop production at once!” the supervisor ordered.
A whistle blew, and the worker bees exited the plant. Soon the bees stopped pollinating flowers, too, because they didn't need the nectar to make the honey.
HONEY
HONEY
NATURAL
HONEY
NATURAL

At first Barry didn't realize what was happening.

Then Vanessa took him up to her garden, to show him how her flowers had died. In Central Park the grass was dead, too.

"This is my fault," Barry murmured. He had to do something—and do it fast—or all the flowers and plants on earth would die.

Vanessa told Barry she was going to the Tournament of Roses Parade in California. This might be the last one ever held.

Suddenly something dawned on Barry: That was the one place where flowers—millions of them—were still alive and contained pollen.

"We can fix this!" he told Vanessa. "We can bring pollen back to New York—and repollinate Central Park!"

At the parade, Barry and Vanessa put their plan into action. They put on costumes, jumped aboard a flower-filled float, and steered it onto the busy freeway. Soon they were on a plane back to New York with the last flowers on earth!

Onboard, the pilot made an announcement. "Our flight has been delayed, folks."

"The flowers have no water," Vanessa exclaimed. "If we don't get home soon, they'll all die!"

Barry decided to take over the plane. Vanessa steered while he gave instructions.

By now the other bees had heard about the plan. The pollen jocks flew up to the plane while millions of bees gathered nearby. On the runway they formed a gigantic flower.

"Aim for the center!" Barry told Vanessa.

The plane hovered above the runway. And then, just like a bee, it dropped into the flower's middle—a perfect landing!

Barry reminded the bees that the flowers contained the last pollen on earth. “So let’s go!” he yelled.

The bee squadron zipped into action, scattering pollen over Central Park.

Barry broke away for a special mission, soaring over Vanessa’s rooftop garden and carefully sprinkling pollen over her dead flowers.

Our plan worked! he thought happily. Soon Vanessa’s garden—and the rest of the world—would be bursting with colorful flowers again!